Four Days in the Life of Zoe Coznaut

Contents

Written by Yvonne Cook
Illustrated by Roger Harvey

Sunday – 1800 hours

I'm feeling ill. Our food unit blew two microchips and our robot couldn't fix it.

Dad said he would cook us some food microbes. I said we should just zap down to McMartians and get two Cosmic Burgers.

Dad said it was no trouble. He told me how much he liked to cook food microbes, from time to time. He didn't think he could forget how to cook. I did!

The last time Dad cooked I was covered in green spots for a week. I told Dad there's no need for humans to cook food. We live in the twenty-first century!

Dad didn't listen to me but this is nothing new. He went off and beamed food microbes in our antique microwave. In no time, a bubbling, green slime was on my food-pad. It was my dinner.

I looked at it and told Dad I wasn't hungry. Dad said some people would be happy to have such a meal. I said he could beam mine up to them. Dad lost his cool and yelled at me to eat my dinner! I did.

Now I'm sick, and so is Dad. Ha, ha, ha!

Chapter 2
Off to Our Solar System

Monday – 0910 hours

Our robot is fixing the food unit. It probably won't work again. Dad still looks very sick but I feel much better.

My school was going on a solar system trip today, but in the end we didn't go. Just as we got on board the school shuttle, Cyril Starwarp got sucked into the shuttle's turbocharger. Cyril was trying to do a trick on his space board. That will teach him to play about.

Cyril's space board jammed the shuttle's engine. Oh no! Cyril wasn't hurt but he was in shock. The nurse gave him two Astros and zapped him to bed.

It took five hours to mend the school shuttle. While Cyril slept, we all had to read the school shuttle safety book. Boring! We were meant to be going on a trip to our solar system.

It's not fair!

Chapter 3
Leaving at Last

Tuesday – 0900 hours

The school is going on the solar system trip, without Cyril. He's still in shock. Suffer! I have my notebook to make on-the-spot reports.

I wave good-bye to Dad.

0910 hours
Blast off. Hooray!

0911 hours
Back to school. Jenny Jupiter forgot her lunch capsule.

1000 hours

We missed the turning for Uranus. We ended up near the planet of Zeon in the system of Zork. The school shuttle driver told us it was just a minor detour. Yeah sure! I think we're lost. Just my luck. I bet the school shuttle driver didn't bring his Spaceways Directory.

1002 hours

Landed on Zeon. Turned up my solar underwear. It's freezing here. I flew up Mount Zeon and opened up my snack of peanut butter capsules. Yuk!

1005 hours

I met a pack of Zeon zombies. They also wanted a snack, my snack! I gave my snack to them. The Zeon zombies didn't like peanut butter capsules either. I flew down Mount Zeon, chased by mad Zeon zombies.

1008 hours

I made it back to the shuttle without being caught, thanks to my jet-propelled boots. I yelled at the shuttle driver to blast off. I think I'm in shock. It was scary being chased by Zeon zombies. I'm glad we've left.

1010 hours

Back to Zeon. We'd forgotten Jenny Jupiter!

1011 hours

Found Jenny. She was behind a rock, stuffing food capsules into her mouth. She hadn't even seen the scary Zeon zombies. Just her luck!

1330 hours

I think the school shuttle driver is off his rocket. He has taken us everywhere. We've been to Mentor on Megus, Tirus on Torus, and Sparton on Spartus, but we haven't been to our own solar system yet. Some trip!

Chapter 5
Our Solar System

1500 hours

At last, we went to our own solar system. I saw Pluto in my video watch. I also spotted a large meteor shower heading our way. I told the school shuttle driver. He thought I was joking and told me there were no meteors near Pluto.

1501 hours

The school shuttle was hit by meteors. I was right. Ha, ha, ha! The shuttle driver had to put up the plutonium umbrella to cover the shuttle. Some of the kids were screaming. What babies!

1502 hours

Jenny Jupiter was sick on my video watch. Not funny. Jenny said she gets shuttle sick. Yeah sure. I said she gets sick because she eats too much. Jenny started to cry. I said sorry, but my video watch will never be the same again.

1505 hours

We headed home. Hooray!

1600 hours

Arrived back at school. All the parents were waiting to pick up their kids. Dad wasn't there. Just like Dad!

Chapter 6
Run Away to Venus

Wednesday – 0800 hours

I didn't talk to Dad all last night. I waited for him at school for an hour. He said the school shuttle was due at 1700. Yeah, sure! I think I'll run away to Venus. Then he'll be really sorry.

0810 hours

Dad just brought me breakfast in bed. Pancakes and syrup capsules, the ones I like best. Dad said that he would take me to Lunar Park on the moon, on Sunday.

Maybe I won't run away to Venus after all!